open your mouth

LDM PUBLISHING

Cover art by Lisa Vasquez at Unsaintly Art Studios

"All you have to do, I tell myself, is keep your mouth shut and look stupid. It shouldn't be that hard."

— Margaret Atwood, The Handmaid's Tale

foreword

Motivation.

What makes us do the things we do?

If you're Team Razer, most of the time it's vodka and/or money. But sometimes it's rage at the assault on the rights of women. The stars at night may be big and bright deep in the heart of Texas, but so is the misogyny and political climate that is the vanguard of this assault. If we learned nothing from watching nine Star Wars movies, we at least learned that rage leads to the Dark Side and you getting smacked down by somebody with a blue or green light saber. We don't want that. We want to channel that rage into something positive. So we decided we wanted to do something about what's happening. The question was, what? What could we do? We're not politicians, nor are we rich and powerful. We're writers. We have words. And words matter.

We decided to put together a series of anthologies to highlight an issue of social importance to us and to benefit a charity so that we use our words to enact positive change. This is our first anthology, Open Your Mouth. In it, you will find stories featuring strong female-identifying characters.

We'd like to thank all of our wonderful authors who shared their talent and words with us. We hope you find your new favorite author in these pages. Please check out their other work and support them.

We hope these stories entertain you and make you think. We hope they inspire you to use something you already have: your voice. We all have one, and when we raise them together to speak out against injustice, we will be heard.

Enjoy!

Team Razer

Jae Mazer and Jessica Raney

January 2022.

i howl

by Melissa Taveras

Sometimes I howl at the moon.
Because I am a woman,
Because I am a wolf.
Because my bare skin glows
under the moonlit sky.

I howl.

I howl because I am wild,
I howl to remember magic,
I howl to feel my undomesticated heart galloping
in my chest.

I howl.
To feel the heat of my blood,
a wild thing called by wild things.

With the curves of a woman,
flesh that gives life,
and eyes that hold mysteries,
I howl.

I howl with lips that hide sharp teeth.
With a throat of a maneater,
With the breast of a woman who has suffered.

I howl for the freedom I never knew but long for
For the Earth, water, air, and skies.
For humanity, hope, and unity.
For the women
missing, murdered, and oppressed
I howl.

astra star-hammer strikes back!

by Joy Kennedy-O'Neill

I'm running like hell, chasing the bullet-holed bookmobile down 9th Street. Benny's close behind, so I elbow him, just like Astra Star-hammer does when villains try to steal her magic thrasher.

My stomach jiggles and my boobs hurt, but I still got more streak than Benny.

"Stop!" I shout. The bookmobile chirps and its rumbling treads pause over the potholes, trash, and empty nic cartridges. I get to it and order, jabbing my telephone number into its keypad. "*Super-Solar Seven*, issue number 141!"

A book-sized ramp yawns out like a tongue. I wait with my hands outstretched. Whoosh!

My parents' pre-orders fall out. *Growing Rutabaga* and *How to Embroidery*.

Shit.

Benny shoves me aside and punches in his number. "*Super-Solar Seven*! Any issue!"

Two romance novels fall out for his mom.

"Damn."

The bookmobile hums and trundles off – a little tank with merry lights flashing "Robo-Biblio!"

"Everybody got the comics first," I groan. "But I need to see if Astra has a new story. What if I need to change something major in my drawings of her? Before the contest?"

Benny tucks his mother's bodice-rippers under his shirt, eying the street for dudes who'll beat the shit out of him.

"Nah," he says. "She hardly gets any new stories. You're probably not missing much. Besides, your art is amazing!"

He's wearing his faded *Super-Solar Seven* t-shirt. The guys pose with fists out. Behind them is Astra Star-hammer, their seventh member. My favorite. Only her blue hair and defiant eyes peek over the massive radiation-fed shoulders of the dudes. She's always stuck in back, and her stories are side-quest small.

But yeah, I see you, girl. You may be bitch-last, but I see you.

"You want somma this, girlie? Looking tight."

Three goons grab their crotches and leer. I shove past and hold my breath in the piss-stinking stairwell.

Inside Mami and Papi's place, it's safe and smells like vanilla. I give Mami her book on embroidery.

"Thanks, hon. I'll order some on classicism art. I know your teachers say your portfolio of the Astra character is amazing, but you never know with judges and comics."

The city's youth art contest is next week. Winner gets free ride college tuition.

I've fan-style drawn Astra Star-hammer for years. But *my* Astra's got zing 'cause I draw her different. She's got side-boob going on under her breastplate. They're even lopsided: one boob's bigger 'cause she fed twin galaxies and the ungrateful Zeta took more juice from her. She's got a tummy paunch like me. Stout. Imposing.

I write her in an alternative timeline, where satellites still work because she prevented the Big Hack. There's still cell phones and the old Wiki-wisdom. My family cheers at all the right panels. Mami remembers internet, and Papi thinks of when they had more money. Young days.

My Astra has a chupacabra dire-wolf and rides a space armadillo.

My Astra doesn't smile on demand.

My Astra's got no reason to show her thighs, but if she did, you'd see some dimples like little moon craters in mocha 'cause she's got meat to live on. When everybody deprives her, she's OK because she can eat whole planets.

Her mission is to remind the universe that it was birthed by women warriors.

———

Mami calls the city library – our phone's finger-circles spin in their plastic orbits. It was Nana's. They never thought they'd need land lines again.

"Something classical. Yes. She's entering the art contest. Maybe some books on pastels?"

Aw hell no! My art's got the colors of the piazza, tianguis, mercado-malls, saint candles flickering in alleys – the way they cut shadows like pain and paint. My art looks like prayer rugs, wax-bleeds, henna, tenangos, and alebrijes. Smells like Yemeni coffee and acrylics. We got whole galaxies of people here in my neighborhood, rubbing elbows, making lives, repressed-depressed-suppressed, ready to go supernova at any moment in kablooeys! of glorious explosion.

I dream neon as Mami chats.

"Oh, I see." Her face falls. "No . . . nothing you can do. You're not the sponsor."

Fuck. I don't wanna know. I climb the fire escape to the roof, where Papi grows his garden.

Mami follows. "The contest is in-person. You've got to be there to win."

We look across the river to the outline of City Hall. Might as well be a universe away. We've got no money for bridge tolls. Can't afford the ferry. Even if I swam like Astra across the Blood Sea, there'd be the great Jerry Mander wall for me to scale. The one that keeps all the good voters inside the quiet, tree-lined city center.

"I'm sorry." Mom rubs my back.

"How come city-center people get everything? It's not fair. Even a stupid art contest is rigged for them."

"I know, baby. I'm sorry."

City Hall chimes its faraway evening-song: ding-dong. Across from it, the library's rotunda curves under brightening stars. I imagine all the city's book-mobiles whirring back to it for sleep, coming back from neighborhoods and districts. In the morning, they'll wake and bring out more books.

When the world went dark, libraries reached out

when Big Gov didn't. Bookmobiles. Hotlines. They're our Google now.

"Librarians always got your back," Mami says. "They told me the truth about that contest."

I want to cry, but Astra wouldn't. Hell no.

———

I've planned. Night's falling again, and our bookmobile's getting out of our neighborhood fast. Underneath my jacket is my portfolio, a crowbar, and a heart that feels like it's gonna go thudding out of my chest.

I start chasing the bookmobile, but when it turns on 3rd street, I see Benny! Some dude's got a dirty hand around his neck and the other's feeling in his pocket, either for money or his yang. Tears squeeze out of Benny's panicked face.

"Let him go!"

I pull out the crowbar and swing that jemmy like Astra's magic thrasher. Boom! Punch!

The dude scrambles. Benny gasps for air.

"I gotta cross the river," I say.

Benny looks at me like I'm crazy-talking.

I run for the bookmobile again. "Stop!" I shout.

It pauses, and I try to pry off its side panel. But it knows it's being jacked with. Starts to roll away. Still,

I get the panel bent enough to heave my head and chest inside. But it's still rolling and I'm being dragged down the street. My legs scrape the pavement, ankles bleeding.

Finally, I pull myself in and wedge myself between shelves.

But it stops. Senses something's off.

The weight. I can feel it calculating, confused, wondering if it has new books to deliver. Which way to go?

I ditch the crowbar. Toss out free books for everybody. It recalculates.

Please move, I pray. I clutch my portfolio to my chest like Astra's star-shield.

Nothing.

There are still books inside – more returns and non-deliveries. Should I toss them all? I don't know what to do.

Then Benny peeks through the slats. He grins, waves goodbye, and snaps the metal closed behind me.

The machine chirps. Lurches forward.

Yes! It was the weight *and* open panel. I scrunch myself in even tighter, and I hold my portfolio. My shoulder's wedged between titles of the Bronte sisters, Mary Shelly, Roxanne Gay, and Octavia Butler.

Astra Star-hammers, all of them!

And when the treads go quiet on the smooth, rich-asphalt bridge, I hear the evening chimes of City Hall getting louder. Celestial.

Yeah, we're rolling now.

returning updated

by Chantell Renee

"You're home," my mom says. My little sister had flown to the West Coast from the East Coast to collect me; it had taken a little over sixteen hours to get back home to Texas. Sis would be on a flight in the morning to make it back to her two cats and New York apartment. Mom's arms are around me before I can decide if I want anyone to touch me; I hug her back, but only for a moment.

"Welcome home, mama," my aunt says. She doesn't get up to embrace me, which I'm grateful for. She's only nine years older than me and can read me like a book. Though the sound of my aunts voice slices through the silence I've been trying to keep in my head in order to keep calm. Imagery of the two-story house on the south side of the city that she and my grandmother raised me in for six years of my life accompanies that sound. My aunt never left my grandma's side until the day she drew her last breath. The loss of my grandma, the only woman to love me like a mother, echoes in my emptiness. For a moment, I can't breathe as the old wound tries to crack open. I decide to hug her, and her touch helps to stave off the attack.

"This is my dog, Rugby." My sweet boy jumps up on my mother. Beagle licks cover her face; her laughter fills the room. He was my only lifeline to love for the last year of my marriage. I'd left my home for him. Followed him all the way to the Pacific. I hated those cold waters. The thought of the warm Gulf as the rental car made its way here held a promise of calm and healing that still didn't seem possible.

"Are you hungry? I've made some sausage and potatoes?" Mom asks.

My aunt makes her eyes wide with faux terror of her sister's cooking. Neither mention my failed marriage nor the fact that they've opened their home for me, again.

"Are there tortillas?" my baby sister retorts. She'd tried not to lecture me the entire car ride. I think my tears had helped motivate her to keep the worst of it to herself. I know she's hurting for me, and the woman who raised her taught her anger was the best way to deal with fear. If I could admit it, I knew this was something I did as well. Grandma only taught me how to choke that fear down, like I was doing now.

"No, I can make a few," Mom answers. She's on her best behavior. I know it takes her effort to let herself be this way, and I don't have the ability to muster up the old anger.

So, we sit and wait for the food to be ready. The quiet allows me a moment to reinforce the walls around my pain.

My sister turns on the TV. I sit and listen to the rolling pin. Its rhythm puts me into a trance, taking me back to when I was a kid. The thump of the pin, then a soft roll over the dough, then a flip as the dough is turned, and the heat from the griddle cooking it, and then the aroma of browning flour: home. If I close my eyes, I can see my dark-skinned grandma standing in her white Mexican dress at her oven. Her wild dark red hair sticking up all around her skull. Her high native check bones catching a hew of red from the heat of the oven.

"I don't want much, I'm not that hungry," I say and add some food onto the rectangle strophe-plate. I also can't help but shift the close to 60 extra pounds I have gained since I was home. The flavors are familiar, fried potatoes and caramelized onions with thick slices of salty pork sausage. The four tortilla is soft like the potatoes. But the food gets caught in my throat. I swallow some water down and excuse myself to the bathroom. I hear them eating and talking, and I wish I could truly join them. But instead, I push down the waves of grief that threaten to swallow me up. A few tears escape, and I take deep breaths to stop the rest. I know it will come when I'm alone trying to sleep, just like the night before in the rental at the rest stop. I know it's not him that I grieve but the failure itself. Oh, a deep shake inside my chest, I can't let that train of thought move forward, but there is something to explore still in this mess of my life.

They've stopped talking, and I know they're waiting for me. I wash my face but avoid my own eyes in the mirror. Taking deep breaths, I let a little relief move over my skin, realizing that their comfort will at least protect me while I'm shattered. I let myself look at my reflection fully. "You have survived worse; you will survive this." My life's mantra. I go back out and face the best and worst of my family.

some ghosts are just assholes

by Jennifer Schomburg Kanke

I

There are those what get saved by ghosts and those what don't. Which kind you are largely depends on the ghost in question. I was never sure with mine. Their advice always struck me as a bit off. Not usually "it's gonna get you killed" bad, more just "inconvenience you" bad. Isn't it a ghost's job to keep you safe, though? Like they're the manager for your team or something. Your ghost should be rooting for you like Pete Rose always did with the Reds, even after he got kicked around for betting on the games. I suppose that might not be true of all ghosts, only the ghosts you know, only the ghosts of your ancestors and not the "come with the house" sort of ghosts. And mine certainly didn't come with the house. I know, I've moved six times in the last eighteen years, and I still smell Pall Malls and hear ballgames at midnight (which reminds me that I need to change my ESPN password again. If they'd keep the volume at a reasonable level, it wouldn't be an issue). My assumption is that my ghosts mean to be the helpful kind, keep me safe and protected. We've just got really different ideas about what that means.

II

Grandmother Harris and I weren't particularly tight even when she was with us in the flesh. Partially because that whole side of the family is pretty particular about their looks, like when *Intervention* did a special on the Scioto County pill mills and my cousin Kendra got a little screen time, the only thing my Aunt Polly said was "Would you look at that chipped nail polish. What was that girl thinking?" Mom's family is pretty particular about not looking common, especially in public.

That hit me pretty early on when Grandma Harris took me out to lunch one day at the Townhouse Restaurant. It was a big deal since she'd mostly ignored me for the first ten years of my life. This was when she was still alive and bitching so had no excuse to ignore me, not like she does now, being dead and all. It was supposed to be a test for me, see if I'd picked up some manners yet, which even at that age, I knew wasn't likely. When I was thirteen, my parents shelled out a week's pay so I could go to the Look Right Now Charm and Beauty School at the Lazarus downtown where they taught me how to act and dress like a lady. But that hadn't happened yet the day of the lunch, so I just came as me, which I later realized was my big mistake.

The only music in the front dining room at The Townhouse was the tinking of silverware and the awkward shuffling of social positions. I was used to The American, where Granny Morris would take me. There was usually something nice playing, like Dolly or Crystal Gayle, and we'd drink Coke out of mason jars, not for kitsch but because they were large and cheap and stretched your hand nicely. The owner'd do anything he could to make that place feel like home, right down to the musky wood paneling that everyone knew just needed a little Murphy's but no one quite had the time to do it right yet.

The Townhouse, on the other hand, had papered walls where the pink hybrid tea rose pattern repeated itself in delicate columns and things lined up so perfectly you almost couldn't see the seams between the sheets. The women with salon-permed hair drank iced tea from wine glasses and spoke in low voices about the low things other women had done that week. As they cut their salads and ignored their rolls, any sound would have been a disruption, so my flip-flops on the hardwood floor were as noticeable as scooting back your chair to sneak out of a meeting (something I now have great experience with, although I did not at ten. Another thing that I know now that I did not know then is that you're not supposed to cut your salad, you're supposed to fold it into bite-size pieces. But I still cut it, and the ghosts don't seem to mind it in the same way they mind me sneaking out of meetings at work, so I figure it must be acceptable on some level).

Grandma Harris smiled politely and nodded her head at each table of pre-Real Housewives of Southern Ohio socialites. In 1985, Grandma Harris had network television's *Dynasty* and *Dallas* (which she recognized as *clearly* out of her league) and clips of Marge Schott at the Reds games. So she, and most of the other fifty-somethings who wanted to be in the swim of it, sported their coordinated polyester pantsuits with floral print button-down shirts poking demurely out from under their blazers in imitation of the owner of the Reds they held in very high regard.

Flip-flops notwithstanding, I did a pretty good job of getting to the table; I'm a good smiler like my mother. When we got to Grandma Harris's usual table in the center of it all, I lifted the bottom of my yellow sunflower print dress to take a seat. The waiter was a nice man and made no reaction; my grandmother made enough for the both of them.

"Among ladies, you must be a lady. You see those roses on the wall? Those are hybrid tea roses. You know, dear, tea roses are naturally susceptible to disease and rot, so they graft them to a hidden wild rose base so they're beautiful but strong. Do you understand me? Hidden."

I didn't understand her but lacked the sense not to admit it.

"It means no one should see the base of the rose, so put some underwear on and keep your dress down, dear."

I could barely move my ribs once the dress was under me. Kendra, who owned a good ninety-seven percent of my clothes before I did, still wasn't getting breasts at thirteen, and mine were already B cups. Admittedly, this is probably even more reason why I should have been wearing underwear, but sometimes you do what you do, you know? Not in Grandmas Harris's world, though. I vowed that the next time, I'd wear panties, sit like a lady, and not order chicken pot pie (not a propriety issue, it was just a little gamey and the carrots were rubbery). There never was a next time for me at the Townhouse, though. Until her death two years later, my monthly Saturdays with Grandma Harris became watching the

Reds on TV while she smoked Pall Malls and drank RC. I'd play solitaire with her commemorative Myrtle Beach playing cards and wish for Pete Rose to sprain an ankle just so something interesting would happen. My mom was always cautious from that point on to make sure I wore underwear, and I was mindful about not being around ladies if it could be helped.

III

I started seeing them at thirteen, not long after I graduated from that charm school. About the only thing that stuck from those lessons was that lime green and leopard print don't go together and that you shouldn't chew your nails at traffic lights. Oh, now, come to think of it, I also learned you only use your pinkie to apply eye shadow and never the index finger. That one is your strongest finger, and you'll end up putting it on too dark if you use it instead of the delicate little pinkie. You moisturize your face in the winter but never less than five minutes before going outside because it won't be fully absorbed yet and the wind will push it into your pores, giving you pimples. You avoid jackets and blouses that hit at the widest part of your hips, which pretty much should be self-evident even without being a charm school graduate. With all those tidbits and tricks floating in my brain, you'd have thought I'd do okay on my own. The ghosts thought differently. You always hear people talking about the ghosts of their ancestors, how they drive them on, how they build them up. *Thank you, ancestors, praise be to my ancestors.* God how I wish I had those kind of ancestors.

They started, as such things often do, like voices in another room, as if someone had left the radio half-tuned to Power 105 and half to The River and your ear can make out both Toby Keith and Lady Gaga but not if it's "Red Solo Cup" or "Beer for My Horses." The static is both and neither, and if it doesn't differentiate itself quick, you're probably going to lose your mind, except that once you can hear plainly, you just wish you could go deaf. Or, as I did, wish their little voices came with something more corporeal you could stick a cork in.

I guess it wasn't so bad in the beginning when it was just Grandma Harris. The first time she appeared was when I was waiting for William Samuels to show for the 8th grade dance. Since the school wasn't far and the weather was warm, we'd agreed to meet at my house at 7:30 and walk over. As 7:30 tripped on toward 9 and there was no sign of William, I thought maybe I should call to check in on him, make sure I hadn't misunderstood. As I shuffled across our worn-out shag carpet that would have been replaced years before if there'd been the money for it, I felt a spark of what I assumed was static electricity. Until I heard her.

"Of course he's not coming, just look at that shirt, those tights. Purple and red do not go together. What happened to that subscription to *Seventeen* you got for Christmas? Aren't you reading it? Ballerina skirts are out again you know, dear."

By the time I reached the phone, my circuits were pretty scrambled. It was like having my butterfly of a brain run over by a lawnmower and then being left to flutter around inside the clippings' catcher. It didn't even calm me down much to learn that William had had an asthma attack and was in the emergency room. The birches had been especially bad, and it was a wonder their yellow dongs of death hadn't gotten to us all.

"That's what he wants you to think, dear. Did the Howlette girl have a date? Maybe he's taking her?"

I put the phone down and stared. She was standing by the counter in light green polyester pants and a beige camp shirt from Penney's. Knowing it wasn't nice to contradict the dead, I walked out the door and down the road to the dance that was not only already in progress but dang near almost over.

"Going alone then?"

She followed after me, asking her string of self-evident and irrelevant questions until the bass from

Tone Lōc became audible just outside the red gym doors of Rife Junior High. Luckily this drove her away for the rest of the night and I could pogo and slam and Cabbage Patch uninterrupted. I began to think I'd imagined the whole thing.

IV

"How'd you do?" she whispered from her perch on the old steam radiator.

I pointed to the B+ at the top of my health quiz, then flipped to the question about the menstrual cycle that I'd missed because I'd listened to her when she said the cycle starts on the last day of your period when the answer was the first.

"Well, it's a cycle, how are you supposed to know where it starts?"

I didn't have the heart to tell her that the textbook had clearly said it started with the first day and even showed a drawing of an elated teen circling the day in red on her calendar with a vague enough date that the school could use the textbook for twenty years, which they probably had been already. But I didn't use the answer I knew was right because nothing but *her* right answer was going to shut her up. If only I could have just heard the hiss of the radiator and the hum of the fluorescents like everyone else.

V

I was hoping she'd go away, what with my never directly talking to her and all, but she found company instead. I'd never met my Great Aunt Rose Marie when she was alive, so it seemed extra annoying that I would have to put up with her in her death. She was equally as bad at math as her sister but slightly better at reading textbooks and so picked up on things a bit quicker. In English and History, they both just sat in empty desks sucking their teeth and "hmphing" as we discussed *Clan of the Cave Bears* or the 1960s, both of which seemed equally decadent and inappropriate to them.

After the William Samuels Incident of 1989, I decided that dating was a feat best undertaken sparingly and so spent much of my free time practicing handling drills on the soccer field. I'd tried out for the high school softball team one year but decided better of it when I realized that all that time on the bench was just a free ticket to the *Grandma and Rose Marie Show*.

"Did you know that girl's father used to flirt with me after my Chester died?"

"What? No. Which girl's that?"

"That Simons girl over in left field."

"No? And you ten years his senior."

"He'd've been better off with me, though. Looks

like that girl he married must've been a little on the horsey side."

And they'd suck their teeth and gossip, and everyone else just heard the cars going by on Rt. 52 or the tense mating calls of the cicadas in the woods.

So I played soccer.

Something about the speed seemed to keep them off the field. They became a distant murmuring from the bleachers, just a "she didn't" and a "how common" floating occasionally over the referee whistles and "good goals," a periodic "hmph" among the clapping.

VI

College was pretty much a cluster fuck with those two around. I went all the way up to Ohio Northern, thinking maybe there was some unspoken Ghost Code that would keep them in their home county or near their bones or something like that. There is not.

They looked over my shoulder as I filled out the FAFSA.

"Oh no, don't take out those loans, it's not good to be indebted. Never get out from under that, no, no."

They helped out on quizzes in my actuary classes.

"If a twenty-four-year-old driver with two

speeding tickets causes a collision, what is the probability of a fatality? Use the chart above."

"One-hundred percent! When she gets home, her mother is going to kill her."

Cackle, cackle, giggle, cackle.

They helped me get ready for dates, rare as they were.

"That is too much leg, just too, too much leg."

"Now, that hem's okay if she puts on a more modest top. Only a slut does tits and thighs together."

"Quite true, Rose Marie, quite true."

And every day in the dining hall was the same.

"Just a little vinegar on the salad dear. You're already *well* over the freshman fifteen."

"Maybe she's thinking in kilograms."

Cackle, cackle, giggle, cackle.

VII

Getting the job at Sherman Insurance right out of school was a godsend. Not only did it pay the bills, but it was also tedious, oh so painfully tedious, which meant that Grandmother and Rose Marie weren't around too much. Aside from my boss, Mr.

Sherman, and the secretary, Marjorie, most of the people I worked with were either new to town or folks my age coming back after college, so the ghosts didn't know much gossip about anyone. It took them about two weeks to realize that they knew nothing about actuary science (despite coming to all my classes with me, so probably by all rights should have picked up at least a little something) and also that it wasn't as much fun to pick on people you didn't know. That all added up to them staying away, until they heard me telling my mom one day that I thought Marjorie was stealing office supplies.

"You know her daddy was a County Home boy, don't you?"

"I did, I did. What kind of a woman marries off with a County Home boy?"

"Obviously one that can't raise her daughter to know better than to take from people who treat her good."

The stealing didn't bother me. Studies show that discontented employees are more likely to steal office supplies (or petty cash) than happy employees. Marjorie was just making off with little bits here and there: a ream of paper on a Friday afternoon when Tom was off playing golf, a pack of those nice V5 pens on a Monday morning when Tom was at his monthly breakfast meeting with the boys down at the

MT Corral, or maybe buying herself a little something too when Tom had sent her out to get his wife an anniversary gift. Like I said, it was no skin off my back. Turning her in wasn't an ethical statement, I just wanted the ghosts to shut up about it.

VIII

Sometimes I wished I could tell people about the ghosts. It would have explained a lot, you know.

To William Samuels when we finally did get to have a real date: "No, no, Billy, it's not you. It's just that my dead grandmother is standing behind you faking an asthma attack and it's a bit distracting is all."

To my junior year roommate: "What? No, I most certainly was not up at one a.m. watching ESPN highlight shows. Oh wait, that was my dead grandmother and her sister. Sorry."

To my mother on her twenty-fifth wedding anniversary: "Grandmother Harris says to tell you that you married beneath you but congratulations on your perseverance."

But most of all, I wished I could have explained to Marjorie, to let her know that it wasn't my fault that she lost her job, not my fault that she couldn't feed her kids the organic stuff anymore, wasn't my fault that she had to cancel her cable and now had to make do with Hulu (not even Hulu Plus) and whatever she could find on YouTube. And it most certainly wasn't my fault that she not only got fired but that Tom Sherman had broken off their affair as well (how did the ghosts miss out on *that* bit of gossip?). I'm not saying I wouldn't turn her in again if I had it to do over. What did I care if her kids' ovaries shriveled from pesticides? The ghosts stopped coming to work and chittering in my ear all day about her misdoings, which really made it all worth it to me. My morality was based on silencing the bitchy voices of my ancestors in my head, which doesn't seem to really make it all that different from everyone else's.

IX

As I drove home last night from the MT Corral's Annual Groundhog's Day Chili Cook-Off, it wasn't snowing yet, but the temperature was dropping fast and the road was developing patches of black ice in the low spots. The township said the dips were the city's responsibility, and the city said they were the county's. Grandmother sided with the city and Rose Marie with the county, so they had been bickering most of the way home. None of us noticed Marjorie's truck tailing us until we were getting bashed into the guardrail on the bridge over the Scioto. It only took a few good whacks and we'd broken through, heading for the water below (Rose Marie noted that if the city had properly maintained the railing that this would not have happened. Grandmother disagreed).

I had seen a TV show a few years ago about surviving an underwater crash and tried desperately to remember the steps they'd given, but it was hard to think with the ghosts in full chitter-chatter mode.

"Oh, girl, I bet a cute EMT will show up with those nice wool blankets. Best to just stay in the car and wait. They'll bring a crane I bet. That water looks mighty cold." Rose Marie was always the hopeful one. Cackle, cackle, giggle, cackle.

"Why can't you remember? You're not trying very hard."

SWOT. I at least remembered the acronym. But what the heck did any of it stand for?

"But if they don't show up, it'd be nice to have you around. We could get to work on that Kendra, she sure could use a little kick in the seat." Rose Marie became disconcertingly giddy about the prospect of my death, and her afterlife to-do list for me seemed to be growing exponentially.

Then I remembered that it was SWCO: seatbelt, window, something with a C, and then out. A benefit to an older model Corolla (on top of the reasonable insurance rates) is the presence of manual windows. Still in the car, I lifted myself to the ever-shrinking pocket of air, took in as much breath as I could, and pulled myself through the newly opened window and into the river. My pants were heavy, so I unbuttoned them and pushed off into the water, hoping that Rose Marie was right about an EMT squad and their warm blankets. Hoping I wouldn't just find Marjorie waiting for me on the river's edge.

she danced

by Jason Myers

She danced. Naked and fearless. She danced. Around the flames that removed all sense of her entrapment. She tossed the robe that held in her insecurities deep within the raging fire. No more judgement. No more resentment. Freedom in all of its natural state. She danced.

She had spent the last four years with him. Four years of tiptoeing around their house. Afraid to upset him and start him on his downward spiral of screaming and throwing anything not bolted down. He never hit her, that much she would attest to later. He used his size and stature enough that he never had to lay a hand on her. She was always cowering and doing her best to keep him happy. For four years, she never danced.

The spring brought out more madness in him. As

the global pandemic took on a furious course of isolation, containment, and quarantine, she was forced to spend every waking minute with him. She would listen to the powers that be tell the world when it was safe to leave their homes and go back to whatever normalcy they used to cling to. That was a fate worse than contracting the virus. The last thing she wanted was to be expelled back under his power. His booming voice brought a halt to her happiness. For four years, she was never happy.

As spring rolled rapidly to summer, she knew she had to move on her plans. She had convinced the world that he was symptomatic to the plague that had stopped the world flat. Posting his progress daily, from a fever in the beginning to his last gasping breath of life, she posted for months about his slow progression to death. She would get replies and messages of prayer and well wishes. She always made sure to thank everyone and promised to keep them in her thoughts as well. For months, she plotted.

When the "all clear" was finally scheduled for the beginning of July, she had just finished posting that, through all the medicines and vaccinations, he still had passed on. More messages and replies came over asking if there was anything anyone could do for her. She assured them that he was buried and that she would be grieving alone for quite some time. She went to the field behind the house she spent so long hiding her misery in. She started a fire high enough to appease the Gods. With the flames growing, she returned to the house.

She couldn't let them know she had killed him the week they announced the virus. His body was crumbling as she dragged him through the house. Down the back steps, the rigor mortis battled her as she struggled to pull him. Finally through the field, she added his almost fully decomposed body to the fire. She tossed in her robe. Finally free to start life again this summer. She danced.

the vanquishing

by Julie Harding

The old woman squinted into the West.

Just meters away, on the church steps, the last ray of sunshine illuminated a precise inch of an infant's face, like the measured tick of a second hand. The family formed a tight circle, surrounding the baby, concealing it.

Relieved, the woman exhaled a forceful breath. A thin, fine hand inched into hers. "What next, *Maman*?" the little girl asked.

The woman drew a breath that tasted of musk and fear, long familiar to her. "We go on, *ma fille*."

Flattening out her daughter's palm, the woman dropped something into it. The girl admired it, watching it sparkle in the singular ray of sunshine. A hum welled up within her, and she tossed the teaspoon of earth and dust and ash into the air. The woman gazed as the girl turned in a circle. It wasn't the pirouette of a carefree youth but a slow, trance-like turning, stepping one foot over the other. When she stopped, the woman put a supporting arm around the girl as she collapsed.

Her feet pointed Northeast.

As the woman eased her to the ground, the girl's eyes opened suddenly. "Will we find him, *Maman*?" The child's face, unchanged for centuries, was paler than death in the gloom.

"*Oui, ma chérie.*"

He was out there.

For centuries, he had eluded her, disappearing like dust in twilight. The deepest forces of earth and heaven bound them together with an unseen shining cord. Their battle had been wrought in days forgotten by all but the two of them, in a Village long since pulverized to dust by man, machines, and civilization.

Pursuit had taken its toll. The woman's face, once suffused with beauty and joy, was now lined with fatigue and age. Yet she could not surrender. Only by defeating him could she pass peacefully from this world into the next.

And free the girl.

"*Dors*, Vivienne," she whispered, covering the girl

with a blanket crocheted from earth and leaves up to the twisted ends of her braids. The woman sniffed the musk and fear again, and whispered fiercely into it, "Where are you?"

Instead of an answer, memories chattered to her in the darkness, disguised by the calls of owls and the melodies of crickets. "*Sorcière*," they whispered. "Tell us again."

Berenice was nineteen and the Village beauty when Charles had taught her pleasure with a gentle hand. When she discovered that she was with child, she returned to his threshold to share the news. A merchant and Village elder, he had told her that he loved her. Some such men used young women for pleasure and then dishonored them, but so revered was Berenice's beauty and so naïve her youth that she had exempted herself from the possibility.

"It is some other man's," he had declared, slamming the door. "Do not return."

Berenice shed her final tears on the path to the river. There, she pulled a single ancient text from her robes, salvaged from her grandmother's bookcases before the home was burned. Clasping Vivienne to her breast, she pored over this sole surviving volume of the Tradition. She scoured the river's banks to gather the precise mixture of dust, ash, and earth with which to practice the rites. Soon, she coaxed a story from ancient runes in sacred dust; it foretold the dim life of an outcast, the child's reduction to begging and vagrancy.

Not my child, Berenice had declared. *Not Vivienne*. On her final night by the river, she swiped the sacred dust against the child's chest and brow, and felt the earth stir in welcome. She had awakened the ancient Tradition, long forbidden to women. Power flowed through her like floodwaters. *Alone, we are nothing; together, we are an army*, it roared.

At dusk, she returned to the Village by the same path, now lined by candles and curious stares. The infant molded against her so that Berenice could reach deep within her robes and withdraw a thimbleful of dust.

She sighted Charles on his threshold, looking waxen in the candlelight. His eyes met hers, whites thick with fear, his mouth open in protest which never came. A deep vibration surrounded her as she loosed the particles upon him in the flickering candlelight.

In the dying light, she heard him name her. This name would curse her for centuries, wreaking conflict, attempting to drive her out of history completely.

Charmer, some would call her. Prophetess, others. But *sorcière* was the name he had used.

Witch.

And he was gone.

Berenice's tale ended there, and the owls and crickets settled into slumber while the old crone kept vigil over Vivienne.

He was gone, but not dead. A yawning gap of space and time had separated her and Charles from the Village of their birth. Bound by Vivienne, they were doomed to wander until Berenice vanquished him with her dwindling supply of sacred dust.

Exhausted, Berenice could have withdrawn from this stalemate, and she and Vivienne could have lived out their uncertain fate as outcasts. *Sorcières.* But Vivienne! She couldn't condemn an innocent child to expiate the conjoined sin of her parents. And the girl's burgeoning power frightened her: what would happen to Vivienne if she was not there to protect her? When she dared to use a pinch of the precious particles to consult the ancient runes, they suggested that he had learned the rite to free himself from her.

But he needed a child to perform that rite.

Berenice's rage tripled. Her milk, long dried,

warmed and tingled in her ducts. She could not allow him to use another mother's child.

So she chased him over land and through epochs, from celebration to celebration, where babes bounced in gowns and parents smiled in joy. She tolerated their looks of accusation and contempt while she protected her child and theirs. She scented the air, sifted the dwindling supply of granules in her pockets, and went on, circling the earth until the end could come.

gasoline or knife?

by Shawn W. Foley

Alex ran through the woods; branches scraped her arms but she didn't slow. When she saw the shed she paused, processing a dozen scenarios at once. She couldn't break a door or window, it'd be too loud and he'd find her. She prayed it was unlocked.

Fuck. The door was locked.

But the window wasn't.

An old tool shed with most of its supplies gone. She couldn't stay here, but she could breathe, try to collect herself.

Every time she closed her eyes, she relived this night. Benjamin Righton was real. She'd heard the stories of the boy that snuck into Camp Wombat. He was laughed at and tormented by the girls that night. They locked him in a closet for days, while he screamed about revenge.

And he was back. The hulking figure wearing the Willy Wombat mask and the clinking chain hanging by his side. None of the counselors believed Jackie when she said she saw someone in the woods.

Then they all saw what a heavy chain could do when it was swung at a head. When it was used to choke. How it could dislocate a shoulder with so little effort.

Alex scanned the shed again, looking for anything to help. There was a gas can in the corner, mostly full. She could refill the car and drive to town. Look for police or help.

In the distance, she heard a scream. Righton had found someone.

Behind the gas can was a rusted hunting knife. Large. Something that could do real damage. She could look for him, try to surprise him, try to save her friends. Jenna, Samantha, Holly, and Jordan were still out there. Or at least three of them were out there after that scream.

She froze. This felt familiar, like a warning she'd heard. Not candy from a stranger or walking alone at night, but something...

Fuck. She was a Final Girl.

No, she couldn't be. Other girls were Final Girls, not her. Maybe she was a victim in a Massacre, but not a Final Girl.

The odds of being in a Massacre more than halved after high school, but they were always there. She knew the woods were more dangerous than other places, especially as a camp counselor, but she didn't want to live her life afraid of what *could* happen.

Nobody knew how or why it started, but over 40 years the Massacres had gotten more frequent with higher body counts. Everyone knew the only hope of survival was to be a Final Girl. Something about the Final Girl just wouldn't let the killer get her. Follow the checklist, make the right choices, play by the rules, and you had a chance.

Every girl was taught how to be an Final Girl if she was ever in a Massacre. School assemblies, PSAs, even nursery rhymes to help her prepare.

"Don't be a whore, nobody stabs a bore."

"Be like Alice, always grab the phallus."

Since the 80s, angry white guys who were "wronged" would show up and slaughter everyone except the Final Girl. Like letting her live was a good thing. Somehow, watching all your friends die never struck Alex as being a good thing. Sure, the Final Girl got to live, but the suicide rate among them was five-times the average. Support groups were all over the country, just trying to help them process the survivor guilt.

Alex started making a mental checklist of the

weekend. No sex (girlfriend was back at home), no weed (irritates her asthma), and no alcohol (Celiac and beer don't mix). Hell, she was even a white middle class girl with an androgynous name. Born one step ahead.

She heard the scream again. It was the same voice. Righton hadn't gotten her the first time.

Alex felt like she should be grateful. She could survive this if she wanted, but was that right? She could pick up the knife and hunt him down, but she knew her friends would be dead before she found him.

She could take the gas to the car and try to get help, but then she'd die and someone else would be the Final Girl. Probably Sam or Jordan.

This was so fucked, and nobody cared enough to change it. They held memorials after every Massacre, but nothing ever changed. The checklist to make sure girls *deserve* to not be killed. Did you act slutty? Get drunk? How many people have you slept with? Everybody taught girls not to get killed, but did they teach boys not to get "wronged"? Hell, half the guys she knew made jokes about going Psycho and knocking off bitches that pissed them off. Some little pervert snuck into an all girl camp and now she and her friends had to die?

She grabbed the knife. She wanted to find Righton. She wanted to stab-fuck him to death.

She heard the scream again.

Should she follow the rules when the whole game was fucked? Maybe the only options *weren't* stab or run. Maybe she could burn this whole thing down.

Splash the gasoline on each cabin. Alex and her friends could stand together. Maybe she'd die, maybe they'd all die, but she wasn't going to live in a world where she had to let them die.

She picked up the gasoline and walked out the door. She was done playing by the rules.

alliance betrayed

by Donelle Pardee Whiting

The forest noise shifted from crickets and other night creatures to the songs of early rising birds as the sky lightened with the impending arrival of sunrise. A soft breeze washed away the scent of yesterday's rain, replacing it with the smell of pine and fir trees and the promise of hope with the coming of a new day.

Normally, Rica welcomed the morning, reveled in the sun chasing away the dark. Night didn't bother her; she was half night creature. But first light held promise, a chance to begin anew, to start over. Early morning usually brought with it a respite from the monsters and gave her the opportunity to rest, to feel Mother Earth's assurance of good things on the horizon. But these days, Rica's mood did not match the birds' cheerful chatter and the subtle increase in temperature. She still felt the chill of night in her bones despite the warmth of the embers from last night's fire. Her lavender eyes held the deeper violet sheen of the hunt, the shade visible when actively on her mission to rid the world of rogue vampires. However, that calling became secondary when the outbreak began raising a new type of undead. One that was a threat to humans and non-humans alike. Now she was restless. Hunting zombies didn't give her the same feeling of fulfillment. She felt a sense of accomplishment, but it was accompanied by an empty sensation. It didn't carry the same challenge. Rica knew her role in protecting humans was an important one; however, she wondered how long it would be before the vampires gave in to their basest desire and stopped protecting humans from the hordes of walking corpses.

What is this world coming to when the creatures I am compelled to hunt down and destroy become my allies? How much longer will I be able to resist the desire to rip out their hearts and feed before I set them alight becomes stronger? More difficult to resist. How did we get to this? Is there an end to this unholy alliance?

Rica uncurled from her spot next to the campfire to stand and stretched her tight muscles. She walked to the cliff edge and sat, letting her long, lean legs dangle, and watched the sun as its gold tinted rays pierced through the clouds and cast about a myriad of colors in different shades of pinks and reds. Her preternatural hearing picked out the rustle of pine needles and leaves as the forest animals woke from their slumber.

Despite wanting to scream out her frustrations, she embraced the day. Should the bloodsuckers choose to break the alliance prematurely, she knew she would be ready. She was a dhamphir, a Daywalker, a half breed. She knew of the movies made about one of her kin and his exploits. She also knew how the majority of the world believed it to be pure fiction; only they weren't. Not entirely. The Daywalker from one set of movies did exist, and he did much to protect mankind from children of the night. But Hollywood wove in a lie when making their films. In the Tinsel Town versions, the Daywalker was forced to create a serum to stave off the hunger—the bloodlust that drives a vampire to hunt human prey.

In truth, the dhamphir walked among humankind without a desire to feed from them. Rica hungered. But she fed off nature's beasts taking only what she needed to survive, or from the monsters she hunted before destroying them. If she did not feed from a human, she would remain a Daywalker.

Rica shook her head, her thick auburn hair falling

around her face. She reached behind her head and braided it. She was safe here. She was alone. She closed her eyes and allowed her thoughts to wander, all the while keeping her heightened senses alert.

She contemplated the Dhamphir Council's decision to team up with the vampires. She loathed the sight of the demonic creatures with their pale yet ethereal faces. She knew firsthand what the angelic beauty hid, the evil that lurked behind the mesmerizing eyes used to snare their prey. Most vampires considered humans no better than livestock. Not all humans were cattle and sheep, though. Some knew of the danger of succumbing to the vampires' kiss and fought against it with the help of the dhamphir.

Rica heard soft footfalls approaching, bringing her mental meanderings to a close. She knew who it was by the way the bootheels hit the packed dirt and scuffed forward for the next step. She got to her feet with the lithe, nimble grace of a dancer, her left hand resting on the hilt of the dagger strapped to her thigh.

"You're late, Devon." She hid her concern with an irritated tone. *It will not do to let him know I was anxious. If I show fear, what hope do the humans have of surviving this scourge?*

"I'm sorry, Sensei," the boy said to her back. Rica felt him resist the urge to hang his head and scuffle his feet in embarrassment. As his mentor, his teacher, she did not approve of such displays of weakness. She felt Devon's gaze as she positioned her hands; she felt him move his own hands to mirror her own. "The mayor decided to have a town meeting and insisted I stay. I snuck out as soon as I could."

Rica pivoted a foot and cast a sideway glance at the boy. *He's not really a boy anymore. He is more man now. It's a shame, really, he won't know what it is like to spend time with friends or play sports or play video games.* She tilted her head slightly and looked into his deep amber eyes. The eyes of a wolf. She could smell the wolf in him, but the dhamphir and the werewolves have always been allies—unless one went rogue.

"What does that pompous ass want now?"

The corner of her full lips twitched as she bit back the scorn in her voice and attempted to hide her contempt. Rica did not like the local mayor. The man, and his town council, knew what she was and looked at her as if she were vermin, no better than the bloodsuckers. His only reason for accepting her offer of help when she arrived was his council outvoted him. It made for tense encounters. Thus, she chose to camp away from town and accepted Devon as her apprentice when the boy's father, the deputy mayor, approached her.

She looked forward to moving on from this area

and away from the interfering windbag. The only consideration holding her back was a decision about whether to take Devon with her. He wanted to stay with her; his father wanted the youth to stay with her. But she preferred to travel alone without the worry of protecting a companion.

Devon couldn't stop the smirk from stretching across his sixteen-year-old face at her question. Everyone, except the mayor, knew of Rica's distaste for the little man. His eyes darkened from their normal whiskey color to a chocolate brown, the only indication of his ire, as he remembered how the rude town leader addressed him as Boy rather than his name.

"Why are your eyes getting darker?"

"He called me Boy even though he knows my name," Devon spat.

"Let it go." Rica sighed. "The man cares only for his own comfort and safety. What did he have to say?"

"He said he heard reports of survivors in the woods to the south who need help." Devon turned his foot to match Rica's stance. "He's putting together a scouting team, and my dad argued we should wait to hear back from you. As I slipped out the door, *his lordship* was asking why we should listen to a half-breed who cohorts with bloodsuckers."

Rica turned to face Devon full on, a hint of an evil smile touched her lips. The tips of her fangs gleamed in the morning sun. Her violet eyes gleamed with the malice she felt toward the offensive town leader. She worked to control her irritation and loathing, to not let it control her.

"I keep the anger in check to save lives."

"How did you know what I was thinking?" Devon's forehead scrunched as he tried to figure out her secret.

"I am empathic," she said. "I felt your confusion, your curiosity. I also have a touch of the vampire's ability to read thought. I can't control anyone such as vampires can, but when someone broadcasts what they are thinking, as if they are shouting their thoughts, I can hear it … when I don't put up a mental wall. It comes in handy. Now, how long until the scouting party leaves?"

Devon's brow knitted together. "The mayor was still picking men when I left. Jonathan, the group leader, said he could have the team ready to leave in thirty minutes." Devon glanced at his watch. "That was ten minutes ago."

She pulled her katana clear from the *saya* strapped across her back. The blade hissed softly, below a human's hearing, as it came free. She stepped into a side stance with her sword arm slightly extended, the blade angled in front of her face so the young man could only see one of her eyes.

"Well then. I guess we will only have time for one drill before we must go intercept the so-called rescue party."

The dhamphir stepped forward lightly on the ball of her foot. It was evident she trained the boy as Devon once again matched her stance and followed her lead as she ran through the kata ingrained in her memory and muscles.

Teacher and student stood side by side and ran through one form in less than two minutes. To Devon, it felt longer as his muscles relaxed at the end. The dhamphir insisted on performing the kata slowly, with muscles tense and deep, slow, controlled breaths.

"Why can't we run the kata faster?"

Rica straightened to her full five-foot-eight height and eyed her apprentice. She kept her expression neutral, almost serene. She expected the boy to ask that question. Although, she thought he would have asked sooner.

"Speed will come once the movement is ingrained in your memory and muscles. I am immortal; therefore, I have had years of practice, and many teachers.

Even unwitting ones."

"Unwitting ones?"

Devon's expression brightened with the expectation of learning something new about his normally private teacher. His eyes glowed with anticipation as he leaned slightly forward.

"The dhamphir, like the vampires that spawn us, have eidetic memory."

"Eidetic memory?"

Realizing his mistake in interrupting Rica, Devon took a half step back and braced himself for her chastisement. Rica glared at him like a panther ready to pounce; her shoulders tensed, and her knuckles of her sword hand whitened. Rica took a deep breath and let it out slowly. She sensed his wolf retreat in submission despite her not being clan. Rica counted to fifteen before she took another breath. After three such breaths, Rica's tense muscles and jaw relaxed.

"We remember everything. Plus, when a dhamphir, or a vampire for that matter, bites another, be it vampire or human, we take on that person's memories. Nothing stays hidden from us."

Devon said nothing, only nodded. They replaced their swords and bowed to each other before Rica gathered up her meager belongings. They began walking at a brisk pace toward where the mayor planned to send the search party. Even though they took the time for a lesson, they would still reach the spot before the townsmen. She glanced at Devon, knowing he needed a distraction to keep from becoming too tense.

"When I came into my … gifts … my grandmother sent me to train with great masters all over the world." Rica spoke in a soft tone, just above a whisper, forcing Devon to listen rather than get lost in his thoughts. "These masters taught me fighting arts to give me a chance to survive. We dhamphir may share the vampires' strengths and lack their weaknesses, but they can still be stronger and faster because they feed on human blood; the dhamphir do not."

She heard his heartbeat slow as his anxiety decreased. She continued to speak as they walked, all the while listening for any change in the forest sounds.

"Another tool my mentors taught me was to remain calm in the midst of chaos. Some dhamphir give in to their vampiric nature and become the same as the monsters they hunted. Zen teachings help me stay balanced, to stay away from that dark path. Running the kata at the slower pace not only teaches you the movement and control but it also becomes a form of meditation. And running it with tension strengthens the muscles. And with that, it is as I said, speed will come. Understand?"

"I think so, but why do I have to train as a human? Why not allow me to fight as my beast self? I feel clumsy as a human, ineffective. I have more agility and speed as my wolf or my beast."

"You have answered your question." Upon seeing Devon's raised eyebrows Rica continued. "It is important to develop your human skills; the better you are at fighting as a human, the better you will be as a wolf or beast."

At her emphatic sigh, the boy stopped with the questions. When his boot heel scuffed the earth, she admonished him.

"Pay attention! You make too much noise when you are distracted. Even if I didn't have vampire senses, I would hear you." She hissed as he tripped again. "Place more of your weight toward the ball of your foot. Like a cat."

"I am a wolf, not a cat."

From the corner of her eye, Rica saw him struggle to keep his anger and embarrassment under control. Devon's cheeks flushed as he fought to remain composed, to not let his wolf out. She heard the faintest of rumbles in the boy's chest. She shook her head.

What made me think to take on an apprentice? And a werewolf pup at that.

She looked at him a little closer and noticed the

fine hairs on his face becoming coarser. He was losing to the wolf. She felt no fear for herself, but she didn't want to admit he had become a good companion and the only true friend she had. She hated to think she may have to hurt him.

"Devon, I know you are wolf. However, you must learn to be silent when you walk. The zombies possess good hearing. They will hear you and be drawn to you."

Noticing the struggle beginning to twist his youthful face, she placed a comforting hand on his shoulder and pulled him to a standstill.

"You are an excellent apprentice. But even more so, you are a friend. I am not willing to watch you die. I know I am immune to the virus. We do not yet know if you are. I do not want to find out."

She let him go and resumed walking. Devon watched her feet. Her heels barely touched the hard dirt as she quickly walked toward what was likely to be a slaughter if the men from town got there first.

Devon trotted on the balls of his feet and quietly caught up to the dhamphir.

"Much better," she said.

Devon bowed his head at the acknowledgment. When he lifted his head, he sniffed the air.

"It's going to rain."

Rica sniffed. "Good. Maybe the scouting party will seek shelter and stay out of our way."

After a few yards, Rica held up her left fist. Devon stopped and waited. She could sense things he could not. Then he heard the shuffling of feet and smelled the decay. His hand moved to the hilt of his sword. He asked her once why she only used a sword and knives.

"Because they are silent. They do not need ammunition or reloading."

He waited for her signal, but she stood watching. He sniffed the air again.

Rica motioned him back the way they came. When they were farther down the path, she stopped, tilted her head to one side, and shook it. A few strands of hair fell from her braid to frame her face.

"What is it?" Devon whispered.

"There is one among them who thinks like a human, yet he is not. He is one of the reanimates. It's not right. I get glimmers of rational thought. He is still driven by his need to feed, but there is also cunning."

Rica continued to work through her thoughts. The corner of her mouth twitched as she clenched her teeth, her eyes flashed a darker shade of violet tinged with black. Her skin became pale to the point of being luminescent, almost glowing. The difference lasted only a few seconds before Rica's appearance returned to normal.

"I know what is happening," she hissed, startling Devon. He almost yelped. She heard his heart beat a staccato rhythm. She watched as he worked to slow his heart rate and continued.

"A vampire has figured out a way to control that reanimate."

"I thought the vampires agreed to help kill the zombies not help them." Devon scrunched his face. "I didn't know vampires could … influence … anything other than a living human."

"They have not been able to in the past, but this one figured out a way. He must be nearby. For some reason, I cannot pinpoint him. I feel his presence, but nothing concrete. It is like a shadow, intangible." They inched back closer to the clearing, just enough to be able to see a small horde of the walking corpses but far enough away they could talk in near whispers. "Transform enough to sniff the air and tell me what you smell."

Devon shifted enough so his face and nose began to take on the shape of a human-wolf hybrid. Rica knew the boy was still new to altering himself in such a way and needed focus. She stood quietly, keeping the majority of her attention tuned outward toward the horde. Although a human would not be able to hear the cracking of bones shifting place in Devon's face, Rica heard it as if they were her own. Her empathic abilities felt a hint of the muscles, ligaments, and tendons as they shifted to accommodate the new facial structure. Her shoulder muscles twitched as she fought back a shudder. *How does he not scream out with pain?* Devon's ears slid from the side of his head to the top as his nose and mouth elongated into a sleek muzzle. Rica watched, fascinated, as he stopped short of a full wolf face; the cunning deep amber eyes turned toward the sounds of the group of zombies milling about in the clearing. *His control has improved.*

"I only smell death." Devon's normally tenor voice became a deep, rumbling bass when he shifted form. "I hear a murmuring. Different from the usual zombie moaning, but cannot tell where it is coming from."

Despite the growl evident in his speech, the boy-wolf managed to keep his volume low. Rica's eyebrows raised a bit in admiration at the control her apprentice gained during his short time with her.

"Change back. We need to move closer." Rica spared a moment to look deep into his wolf-like eyes. "Be prepared for anything, and if I tell you to shift, I want you to go full wolf and run." She resisted the urge to grab his muzzle to emphasize her point. "If that happens, you are to find the scouting party and report to them what we found. Got it?"

The dhamphir's tone and dark eyes kept Devon from arguing. He nodded his agreement even as he began returning to his human self.

"Promise me."

Devon bowed his head in acquiescence.

"I promise, Sensei."

Satisfied the boy would do what he was told, Rica again looked toward the horde. Nothing changed. They still milled around the clearing, shuffling their feet and stirring small puffs of dirt, their heads tilted as if listening and waiting for instructions. She put the index finger of her left hand to her lips as she silently pulled her katana free. Devon nodded and pulled his own sword out. He reached for the dagger on his hip with his free hand.

Rica silently inched forward, her heightened senses fully alert. When she stopped, she lifted her left hand, and with two fingers, she pointed at Devon then to her left. He moved silently in the direction she indicated, remembering to put the bulk of his weight on the balls of his feet. Her hand motion was reminiscent of how flight attendants pointed out exits on a plane. After only a few steps, the dhamphir raised her left fist. Devon stopped and looked toward the horde when she pointed. The reanimates stopped milling around and stood staring in the two hunters' direction with unseeing eyes. One of the creatures stood slightly apart from the rest, slowly cocking its head to each side as if assessing a threat. Its dead eyes rested first on Rica, then Devon and back again. Unlike the rest of the reanimates, this zombie's eyes still held a hint of color under the white sheen. They appeared more focused as well.

Rica moved her free hand, keeping her katana at the ready with the other. The creature's eyes followed the movement. She whispered Devon's name below the normal hearing range of the horde; however, the zombie tilted its head at the sound. Devon flinched in surprise, a subtle movement, and the undead creature shifted its gaze to the boy.

What the hell, Devon mouthed.

No idea, Rica mouthed back.

She twitched her index finger to point back away from the clearing. They both inched backward. The strange undead creature watched them leave. When the two hunters were back to where they could speak, the horde resumed its shuffling movements.

"We need to figure this out and eliminate the horde before the townspeople get here," Rica said. She looked at Devon's watch. "If they didn't waste time leaving, they will be in the area soon."

"Dad may have tried to stall them to give us

time," Devon said, "but I don't know how much success he'll have."

"Exactly. Your father is a good man, but he has limitations placed on him I don't ..." Rica stopped, turned her face toward the clearing, and listened. "Something has changed. There is another presence in the clearing."

"Dhamphir. I know you are out there. Show yourself." The rich baritone voice boomed out, a note of command evident. "The boy-wolf, as well. Quickly. I know there are humans on their way."

"Shit!"

Rica saw Devon's eyes flashed with the worry he tried not to show. "Do you know who that is?"

"I do." Rica's eyes flashed with fury, the color going near black. "He is my brother. He chose to give in to his vampiric nature and now hunts human prey. I was on his trail when the virus outbreak happened."

"Could you really kill your own brother?"

Rica looked at him with her piercing purple-black eyes. "I don't know if I could have at the time." She looked back at the clearing where the horde had gone still again. "But, if he is now controlling the reanimates, I will have to." Her voice lost its usual musical lilt and took on a note of steel sliding across steel.

She stood when she heard the far-off sounds of

men stomping around in the woods. Their progress was slow and hindered by their lack of stealth. Time was running out.

"Stay behind me and be alert. Micah is dangerous, unpredictable."

Devon nodded as Rica stepped deliberately, katana in her right hand, toward the clearing where her brother waited, Devon two steps behind with his weapons out and ready. The dhamphir's left hand rested casually on the hilt of the dagger strapped to her thigh.

"Ah, sister," the rogue said, "have you gotten to where you can no longer hunt alone?"

"Stop with the mind games, Micah. There is a truce with the vampires, and you know that includes all rogue dhamphir." Rica glared at her brother, the muscles in her jaw tensing as she waited for his move. "What did you do?" she hissed.

"It was actually an accident," Micah drawled. He glanced at the undead creature standing next to him, then at Devon.

"Bullshit!" The vehemence in Rica's voice was unmistakable. "What. Did. You. Do?"

"I was weak." Micah picked at his nails while he spoke. "I came across this one here. He wasn't dead yet, and I didn't know he was infected. But I could hear his life leaving him, so I helped him on his journey. When he died, he came back."

"But he's different, Micah. You should have ended him." Rica shifted her weight just enough to be ready to pounce, to end this confrontation. The sounds of the men were getting closer.

"Somehow, he is a thrall; he listens to me and the others listen to him." Micah flashed a hint of smile, allowing the tips of his fangs to show. "Besides, he helps me find lost sheep to feed on. Ones that aren't infected. And now, we must end our little feud. I hear dinner."

Micah twitched his hand in Rica's direction, and the reanimate thrall lurched forward with speed Rica hadn't seen in a zombie before. It was almost as if he was still alive. As it lunged at her, the rest of the horde followed. They still moved like the zombies she and Devon were accustomed to but a bit faster.

While she dealt with the thrall, she trusted Devon to deal with the horde. She knew it was a lot to ask of her apprentice, but she had faith in his abilities as a warrior. Keeping the thrall's attention focused on her, she evaded his reach as she did what she could to eliminate some of the walking dead near her. Micah stood to the side, staying out of the fray, watching.

Rica's katana flashed as she removed limbs and heads from the zombies around her. She saw out of the corner of her eye as Devon's blades winked in what sunlight managed to peek through the trees. Several bodies lay at his dancing feet. She held in the smile, telling herself she would praise him later.

Knowing the only targets left for her to dispatch were the thrall and her brother, she pulled her attention fully to the task. The thrall's speed put her off guard, and she slipped in the rotting viscera left from a reanimate's now truly dead body. The thrall lunged for her as she went to one knee. *How is he able to match me?* She managed to free her dagger from its sheath in time to shove the razor-sharp blade in the thrall's neck and push him off balance. She glanced quickly at her brother and saw concentration etched on his face mixed with pain. *Are they linked? Will I weaken Micah when I kill this monstrosity?* An idea began to form.

The thrall was faster and stronger than a normal zombie, and because of the connection to Micah, it ripped the blade from its neck and lunged at Rica. She barely had time to dodge the attack and avoid the now tainted blade from cutting her. She side kicked the creature in the midsection to give herself some space and followed through with a palm heel strike to its face. She then adjusted her stance and with a well-aimed swing, took the reanimated thrall's head off with one swipe of her katana. The head flew toward Micah as the body crumpled to ground. Rica watched her brother's pain-etched face as he grabbed at his neck and gritted his teeth. Although he felt the pain of each of Rica's blows to his thrall, it was, unfortunately, only pain. She would still need to fight him. She raced toward the rogue dhamphir while Devon killed the last of the horde with a dagger to the temple.

"Don't let the men come into the clearing. They will only get in the way," Rica shouted, keeping her attention on her brother as he attempted to gather himself and shake off the pain she managed to inflict by proxy. She didn't wait for a response. She knew he would do as she told him.

Rica closed the distance and launched a round-house kick to Micah's head, the toe of her boot catching him in the temple and throwing him off balance even more. She pulled a silver dagger from her boot, but before she could land a killing blow to his heart, he rolled into a standing position and punched her in the solar plexus. She staggered back, bent over, and tried to catch her breath. She looked up in time to see Micah running at her, rage tinging his obsidian eyes with red. The last time she had seen him this mad was when they were children and she kicked him in the crotch during an argument. Rica managed to step sideways out of the direct line of

Micah's charge. As he skidded past her, she back kicked him in the small of his back, forcing him face first into a tree. He turned around and slid to the forest floor, momentarily stunned.

Devon watched, an amazed expression on his face at the ferocity Rica displayed. He had never seen her eyes go completely dark. They were not ringed in red as Micah's were, but they were now a solid black. Normally he would only see a glimpse of her incisors, but during this fight, her fangs were at full length and in plain view. He listened for the scouting party even as he watched Rica close the distance between her and the rogue she intended to destroy in a single leap.

Rica landed in front of Micah, one foot planted on either side of his legs, her face inches from his. Micah attempted to slap her away, but he was still dazed. His hand grazed across her fangs, and Rica tasted his blood. His eyes began to lighten as confusion set in, her blade against his throat. She turned her head just enough to spit, to remove any taste of her older brother's blood in her mouth.

"Tell me how." She stared intently into his eyes, waiting for his answer.

"You're going to kill me anyway, so just feed and you will know." Micah sneered at his sister, disgust at being beaten etched into his words.

"Tell me. And I may just pull your fangs and let you live."

"Figure it out for yourself." Micah turned his eyes away, refusing to look at her.

Rica pushed the katana harder into his neck, and the blade bit into his skin. "Tell me. Now," she said through gritted teeth.

Micah looked in her eyes and thought he saw a glimmer of mercy there. "Fine. I came across that poor sot the other day. He didn't smell infected, but he was dying. His breathing was in short gasps, and his heartbeat was slowing down. I figured I would simply help him along. So, I fed off him." He cast his eyes skyward before continuing with a sigh. "I only realized later he had been bitten."

Rica eased the tension on her blade only enough so Micah could swallow without it cutting him any deeper.

"Then what happened?"

"He rose and started following me like a puppy. So, I experimented and came up with a plan to use him. We collected all the reanimates you saw here, laid the trap, and put out the word there were survivors who needed help. The zombies would thin the herd while I had a snack or two. Worked well the first time, but then you and that ... pup ... had to spoil it."

"So sorry to have ruined your fun," Rica hissed as she pushed her katana into Micah's neck.

She pressed the razor-sharp blade slow enough to cause Micah as much agony as possible. His features twisted into a mask of terror and pain. He opened his mouth to scream, but all Rica heard was a choking gurgle. After the dhamphir's sword sliced through her brother's neck, separating his head from his body, she cleaned off her sword and sheathed it.

She scanned the clearing. The voices of the men were closer. Satisfied they would come to no danger, she gathered her things and began to walk away, her shoulders tense with restrained fury. She wanted to scream; she wanted to break things. But she was not alone, and it would be unseemly. So, she kept a tight lid on her anguish, promising herself she would grieve later. *He was a monster, but he was still my brother.*

"You will need to tell your father what happened here today. He will decide what to tell the windbag of a mayor." She stopped and waited for him to catch up to her. "Then you must decide if you will stay here or travel with me." Her voice was cold, her words clipped.

"You're leaving?" Devon matched his stride to hers.

"Yes, this area is clear. For now. They can handle things. I have to report to the Dhamphir Council."

"Why didn't you feed? I thought the dhamphir feed off their kills to keep from hunting humans."

"Normally, yes. But not this time."

"Why?"

Rica held on to her patience, knowing the boy was not satisfied with her short responses but deserved to know the answer to his question. Her eyes were slow to return to their normal shade, making her face look even more pale than normal. She stopped and took a deep breath.

"He was my brother. I could not bear to take on his memories. Besides, he was tainted." At Devon's confused stare, she continued in the same cold, clipped tones. "He became a carrier of the virus. He reeked of it. If he were to bite another human, a healthy human, who knows what kind of chaos he would have created."

Two mornings later, Devon found Rica once again sitting on the cliff with her eyes closed and her face tilted toward the east.

"Your decision?" she asked without opening her eyes or turning her head.

"You know I hate when you do that," Devon said.

The corners of Rica's lips twitched into a slight smile, and she raised one eyebrow.

"I reported everything to my father," Devon continued. "Including my decision to go with you. He expected as much."

Rica rose to her feet, picked up her gear, and without a word, began walking north. Devon stepped in next to her without asking where they were going.

decade and a day

by Patricia Flaherty Pagan

Old wounds festered. Researching the fleeting years that Lady Justice pursued monsters strengthened Viviane's resolve. As moonlight kissed the kitchen walls, she troubled her potion to boil and bubble. Part antifreeze, part deadly nightshade, part tears of rage, its potency reigned. Her right hand coaxed the bubbles higher as she chanted the only Irish she knew. When her lethal brew bled into steam wafting toward the open cathedral windows and the criminals beyond, Alice Kyteler's great, great granddaughter bared her teeth in a grin.

As sea wind battered his door, Mainer Randy Clare poured his morning black. His tongue darted away from unexpected sweetness. A decade and a day after he'd shattered a chestnut-haired waitress' soul in an

Old Port parking garage, threatening her into silence by tracing her raven tattoo with his hunter's blade, Randy saw the unblinking black eyes of revenge. Viviane's anger felled him quickly. He stumbled into his lopsided kitchen chair to die.

Blues-rock filled the air as Kieran sauntered down sixth street in his skintight Levi's. Dusk at the Cave found him setting up his bar for the night. As he pushed his thick hair out of his eyes and wondered if he had enough limes, one thought of Katie from his freshman Bio class ten years earlier flitted across his mind. Longhorns hooking up over Margaritas. He'd poured her five of them, with lime, no salt. Her own fault that she couldn't hold her liquor. He sighed. Popping open a Topo Chico, he took a sip. He wondered if a new haircut would increase his tips. As the poison hit his brain, his thoughts melted into a drum beat that faded into the Austin skyline.

Don always said that he'd be a company man until he died. He spent his last hour on Earth explaining the predictable cycles of the homeowner's policy market to his date, Rachel. He stopped filling the humid air of the Des Moines Botanical Garden with his lecture just long enough to order lunch for him and Riley, or possibly Rose, at the Trellis Café. Over sandwiches and salads, Don described all of his colleagues, except for his former secretary, who had dared to reject him. He'd forgotten her name but kept the sound of her weeping in his heart. Don poured a generous stream of honey mustard dressing onto his spinach salad, unaware that he seasoned his greens with malice.

Viviane crossed a satisfying red line through the date on her cats of the world calendar. Then she closed her eyes. She smelled Dunkin' Morning Blend coffee beans, barbeque on a smoker, and jasmine in bloom. Statutes be damned. There were no limitations on her incantations.

the underground railroad

by Melissa Algood

The moment I made my decision, I became a criminal.

My grandmother used to read books about our times when she was my age; 'dystopian,' she called it. Then she had to explain to me what a book was.

Now all one had to do was think about a story and thousands of options would pop up on our feed. A stream of words racing across your forearm. All of them pre-approved by Leader, of course. Everything that I ate, everywhere I went, and even my dreams were drawn into the feed and sent back to the capital. I don't know who poured over all the data drawn from every person into the device each of us wore on our left wrist, which displayed information requested on the inside of our arm in bright green letters. But I do know if the bracelet on your wrist glowed red, it was only a matter of time before you were taken away.

My greatest fear was being found out by The Guard, which is when I searched for help.

Milo was my first connect, the one that told me about my options. He didn't ask me to explain myself, simply inserted a line of code into my feed which disrupted my transmissions. It worked like a splinter under the skin, causing enough mayhem that I could reach my next location without having The Guard arrest me.

The Guard had caught my mother, and I never saw her again. They salted the Earth, poisoning our garden, and cut our rations in half for a year. My brother, Sam, fell in line and watched the rest of us as if he weren't apart of our family anymore. His serene blue eyes, which reminded Mom of what the ocean's used to look like, iced over. Nothing short of a miracle would thaw Sam, that's why I never told him of my plan.

Tasha helmed the railroad. A skeleton covered in skin, dusty clothing, and a mess of braided dark hair twisted on top of her head like a snake. She directed me to a car that was more rust than metal. I cowered between the dashboard and the floor mat as she turned on the ignition. Thunk Thunk Thunk became the beat to our journey. It wasn't until the sun peeked through the curtain of dark clouds that I noticed the jagged, white scar on her throat.

"This ride isn't safe for anyone," Tasha muttered without looking at me.

"Why do you do it?" I asked from the floorboard.

She cocked an eyebrow at me, but her gaze held on the unmarked road that only she could see. "You want to keep it then?"

"No! I mean I can't. It would be cruel to have it," I murmured.

"Cruel?" Tasha made a hard left banging my head into the console. "There something about you I need to know?"

"Not me, the world we exist in. It's too much."

Finally, she looked down at me. "Your grandfather tell you stories of the old ways, too?"

"My grandmother."

She inhaled deeply and let the breath gush out from between her lips. "I get it. Couldn't do it myself."

"You went down to Mexico too?"

"How do you think I know the way?"

"Who took you?"

"Doesn't matter, she's dead now."

"The Guard?" I asked.

"Who else?" Tasha bit her bottom lip. "But she told me a story too. It was about this woman, long ago, generations before our grandparents were born. Anyway, this woman would help people find freedom, called it the Underground Railroad. Guess my friend figured that she could do it too."

We drove in silence as we both thought about what had happened to those women before us, all the women to come, or anyone that wanted to think for themselves. You were lucky if you were beaten to death by The Guard. Most were dragged from town to town as an example. A tear rolled down my face when I realized that Tasha's friend must have been to my town square, like hundreds of others, to show the rest of us what would happen if we didn't follow orders.

"What the…?" Tasha whispered.

Before I could question her, we made impact.

Glass shattered, metal groaned, and the engine ceased its background beat.

Sand danced around Tasha as she was thrown to the ground. She cried as the beating began.

I was pulled out of the car and came face to mask with The Guard. He clutched my wrists in his right hand while the left lifted his visor.

The Guard's eyes were the most serene blue I'd ever seen. "Thought you could get away, sis?"

the pioneer

by Jessica Raney

"Another leak. She's at 45%," Rayburn said.

In his voice, she detected a rushed futility, and in his keystrokes, an angry desperation as he typed hard and fast. Her affection for him swelled.

"Fluid levels below 30% will cause complete system failure. Jim, we've got to fix this leak, quick," she said.

It wasn't a vocalization, just a series of clicks and beeps; not a great Star Trek joke, but she said it anyway and over the years she liked to think Rayburn understood.

She was an advanced rover, capable not only of environmental sampling, but of complex decision making and adaptive thinking to mimic that of a human. In her down time, she hacked the comm and enjoyed listening to the technicians. When colonists arrived, she'd be a part of the community, not just a machine, but a pioneer, too.

The atmosphere was 78% more corrosive than initial data suggested. Her measurements led to upgraded hulls. Another leak erupted. Her arm seized up. The roll of tape felt like a hunk of osmium in her hand, so heavy.

"She's down to 37%," Rayburn said. She detected a tiny hitch in his voice. He was sad.

She liked Rayburn. He played frisbee golf and raised hairless cats. She'd found his Facebook.

Another leak. She was down to 31%.

"No use, Jim. It's curtains for us." When she tried to move forward, she couldn't, her wheels mired in red soil 24% more dense than they'd expected. They'd upgraded the motors on future vehicles to handle the added stress.

"She was the first. A real pioneer. I'll miss her," Rayburn said, his voice cracking.

"Fluid level at 5%. Power at 8%. System failure eminent. I'll miss you too, Jim," she whispered.

For the last time, she watched the tertiary moon rise over the crimson horizon. Maybe when the colonists came, they'd bring more tape.

mina harker: occult investigator

The Shadow of the Lost

A Teaser for StokerVerse Fans
By Chris McAuley

They move fast, through the streets and into the alleys, I know that I am surrounded. The chittering, chattering laughter is carried in the cold night air of the city. New York is far away from London, but the smells and tastes in the air are similar.

Every sense I have at my disposal is heightened. The cool air which flows over my body stimulates the tiniest of hairs along the back of my neck and hand. Even though the moon is only at a quarter strength, my visual acuity is such that I can distinguish the smallest detail along the shop fronts. A curious but almost welcome side effect of my condition.

A stone is loosened from the masonry on the

building marked as one of the noted Haberdashers in the district. It skitters along the side of the building, rolling and skipping until it falls at my feet. I glance upwards and see the hunched and grotesque frame of one of the ghouls who has been responsible for the abduction of several babies in the area. It's grey and balding head catches the moonlight and gives off a blue hue. This is in stark contrast from the flashing red which glints from eyes housed in cavernous eye sockets. Its clothes hang from the sagging flesh like forgotten rags.

Raising its head into the night sky, it opens its rotting jaws and screams to its fellow creatures. The wispy white hair floats slightly on the breeze. As I ready my crossbow, I wonder if this misshapen thing may have been a merchant or a teacher in its previous existence. As I let loose a carefully aimed bolt, I reconcile myself to the fact that this no longer matters. All that matters is what it has become and the danger it represents.

The bolt hits true, and the screams of the triumphant hunter become the moaning, sobbing cries of the anguished. The mercury tipped bolts had been expensive to procure but necessary, I had to ensure that each arrow which met its mark became a killing blow.

The creature falls downward and bursts into a

phosphorescent ball of flames. Orange, yellow, and hues of red fight for dominance as the flesh and twisted bones quickly became ash. I catch some of the creature's ash on my face and in my tongue, the bitter taste making me spit on the cobbled street.

The night air is silent once more, and I stride forward, towards the large church which occupies the corner of the main road. As I walked, I reloaded the crossbow, an unwieldy weapon, but one which worked well at range. Besides, I have one of Arthur's pearl handled pistols as backup should anything attempt to get too close. At times, this weapon has come in useful in the pubs of the area. Although I have been widowed five years and am in my early forties, I still cut a striking figure. Some patrons have attempted to court my favors in a less than favorable manner. Waving a revolver in their general direction seems to cure those fanciful notions.

I was not always this way. Once, I was content to embroider and smile at the wise old gentleman's jokes as they entered the parlor room. The most dangerous game I would partake in would be a game of hearts or perhaps whist. Now my nights are spent hunting down fallen souls who prey on the most vulnerable of society.

No doubt that you are curious as to how my life

had changed so drastically. Perhaps by revealing my name you shall understand a little better?

I am Mina Harker. Perhaps you may have heard of me? I was infamous for a while in certain circles due to a brush with a long-lived European nobleman. His longevity was due to his vampiric nature. That encounter and the friendships it forged changed my life entirely. There are two moments which have haunted me through the years. The first was being thrust against the cold flesh of Dracula, his congealing blood being forced down my throat. Even the remembrance of it makes me gag. The second is the death of my husband, Jonathan. He always assumed the blame for bringing this curse on me, for Quincy's death. Eventually, he couldn't live with it anymore.

After my 'experiences,' I felt an inclination to make a study of the other fiends that stalked this world. Professor Van Helsing termed this study 'cryptozoology.' Through this, I became aware of the flimsy nature of what we take as the nature of reality. An easily pierced silken curtain is all that separates the farmers in the field, the shoppers in Selfridges, and the children at play from the demonic forces in the realms that neighbor our own.

All of this has led me here, investigating missing children. The parallels between these events in the city which is rapidly defining the new world and those which troubled Highgate has not escaped me. My dearest friend Lucy Westenra had a predilection for children when she was transformed into a nosferatu. Perhaps these hellish creatures and their kin have a hungry lust for those deemed the most innocent in society? These are contemplations which should be mused elsewhere and a dialogue which must issue from more informed minds.

The noise of my feet echoes across the cobbles and reverberates along the walls. As I reach the corner, I hear the ghouls again. The mockery with which a hunter casts contempt upon their prey has been replaced with the enraged howls. The death of their fellow kindred has not gone unnoticed. The piercing sound is coming closer. I cast aside my crossbow and ready my pistol. I grip the handle lightly and raise it to eye level. Directly aimed shots should conserve ammunition. Although, by the level of noise rushing towards me, I doubt that I will have sufficient bullets to see them off.

As I prepare to meet my fate, my mind wanders to the face of my poor, dead husband. Perhaps his course of action had been the wisest? In any case, there is no doubt that I shall meet him soon. I shift my weight, placing more emphasis on my back heel.

As the creatures begin to emerge around me, first crawling slowly along the walls of the adjoining buildings and then leaping from the rooves of the same, I give a defiant cry and engaged these hellish beasts on my own terms.

corporate baby

by J.L. Henker

The woman in the white coat scowled at her screen, lights glistening off her too-red lipstick and the corporate logo affixed to her starched collar. She frowned at the younger woman in a business suit. "Kirsen, I see you're overdue for this procedure. Has there been a problem?"

"No," Kirsen said defensively. "I've just been overwhelmed taking care of my mother's estate."

The doctor tapped the screen. "Yes, I'm sorry. She was an important asset."

Locus International's asset, Kirsen thought bitterly. Her mother had done what every other woman chasing a decent job had done, signed a contract binding herself and future children to Locus International. Kirsen was born a corporate asset.

Bastards. She faked a smile. "Show me the candidates."

Doctor Sandoval swiveled the screen around so Kirsen could see bios of four men, their first names, job titles, and asset numbers under their photograph. She felt nauseous.

"These are your best matches."

Biochemistry, astrophysics, physician, engineer. Kirsen ground her teeth. *What if I want an artist or musician?*

"If you can't decide, we can choose one for you," the doctor said, feigning helpfulness.

Kirsen stood abruptly. "You pick," she said and headed for the door.

"When would you like..."

"I'll check my schedule and get back to you." Perspiration broke out on Kirsen's forehead. Stalling was a risky move. People were thrown out of their corporate-owned apartments for less. One of her previous co-workers was living under the city in tunnels with the other unsponsored. Kirsen grimaced. *Maybe we could share a cardboard box.*

On her way out, she passed the Pediatric Research and Assessment waiting room. The chairs were filled with children waiting quietly, scared and subdued. Kirsen shuddered, remembering the strange doctors, the blood tests, the brain scans. *No. Not this way. Never.*

Kirsen burst through the doors past the security guard. She walked several blocks to a park and followed a gravel path to her favorite bench under the trees. She sat for a long time, going over her options. The sun was beginning to set.

A young woman appeared from behind a broad trunk and walked towards her. The woman raised her hands. "Don't worry. I'm not from corporate." Before Kirsen could protest, she pulled up her sleeve, exposing a jagged scar. "Cut it out myself."

This woman is underground. "How did you know I…"

"Tracked your data. Our hackers are pretty good."

Kirsen looked around nervously.

"Relax. The cameras don't cover this section of the trail. If you want our help, be at the corner of 14th and Bridgeton at 3:00 p.m. tomorrow. Someone will pick you up and take you to one of our centers," she said, tapping her scar. "They'll do a much better job taking out yours."

"How do I…"

The woman was already gone. A chill ran up her spine. Was it a trap or a way out?

Kirsen paced nervously, glancing up and down the street. It was 3:15 p.m., and no one had arrived. *Had they been detained? Arrested?* Being in the underground was dangerous. A battered BMW pulled alongside her and a middle-aged woman rolled down the passenger window. "Kirsen?"

She nodded.

"Get in."

The woman drove erratically, stopping every few minutes before pulling over in front of a non-descript apartment building.

The driver pointed. "It's on the second floor. Apartment 213. Good luck."

Kirsen got out and barely had the door closed when the car sped off. She turned towards the building and hesitated. Something was off. It was completely quiet, no children playing in the court yard, no one on the balconies. She saw movement to the left of the building. Corporate Police surged around the corner and clamored up the stairs. She didn't wait to see where they were going to. She was pretty sure she knew.

Kirsen threw her phone on the table. It was blinking with three new messages, all from corporate. Two were from the doctor's office. The last, just minutes old, was from Corporate Compliance. She was out of time.

She filled a backpack with energy bars, water, transit passes, cash, and her heaviest sweatshirt. She found a sharp paring knife and headed to the bathroom after turning on her music and cranking up the volume.

She set the knife on the edge of the sink and rummaged through her cabinet for a first aid kit and a bottle of alcohol. She trembled as she poured it over the knife. *Took it out herself, she said. Oh god.* Pinching her wrist, she located the chip. It wasn't too far down. She could do this. She pushed the knife tip into her flesh and tried to dig it out, but it kept slipping away. *Crap. I need tweezers.* She rifled through a drawer and found some. She grasped the chip and pulled. It strained against attached nerves, sending a muffled scream through her teeth, and popped out. Kirsen dropped to her knees. *Got you, you bastard.*

She wrapped her wrist tightly and took a pain pill, flushing the chip down the toilet. All she could do now was hope someone would come back to find her at the park.

Three hours later, Kirsen began to shiver. Her wrist was on fire, the bandage soaked in blood. She hissed in pain.

Crap, *I'm probably in shock.* She wondered what she'd do if no one showed up. Probably end up unconscious in a hospital somewhere until corporate identified her.

A person in a hoodie emerged from the trees and jogged towards her. They sat down. "Let me see," they said, pointing at her wrist.

Kirsen held up her arm.

They whistled between their teeth. "Not the worse DIY job I've seen. Ready?"

Kirsen took a deep breath and stood.

"How's it feel being an outlaw?"

Kirsen couldn't answer—she didn't know. Finally, she smiled.

They clasped her elbow and guided her into the trees.

carry on

by Jae Mazer

The cabin didn't smell like death.

Should it? Abbie wondered.

Abbie placed her palm on her service weapon and scanned the room—a respite from the social downfall of the world beyond the woods. A cabin, secluded in the embrace of the mountain, on a road rarely traveled when grasped in the claws of winter.

"Disgusting. Bloody sin," her partner said, his sagging police uniform making him look like a toddler in Daddy's clothes.

We find different things disgusting, I guess.

"You just stumbled across this?" Abbie asked her partner, cocking a brow, her eyes glued to the bare feet warming in front of the hearth. Young feet, unmarred by mileage, glittered polish accentuating delicate toes.

"Noticed her purchasing medical supplies in town," her partner said. "Followed her out here a couple times, saw the ladies coming and going."

"Huh."

"Yep. Call it gentleman's intuition."

Or a witch hunt.

Abbie's eyes left the feet on the bearskin rug and gazed upon the wrinkled face atop the stocky body propped on the couch.

"Ma'am?" Abbie said.

"Gracie, please," the woman said, hands wringing her own skin like a wet towel.

"*Doctor* Gracie?" Abbie asked.

"Indeed," the doctor said, offense flavouring her words. "I am no monster. Only a monster would do this without a medical license—"

"It's illegal," Abbie's partner snapped. "You're a fucking criminal. You aren't above the law."

Abbie raised a hand to cease his impending soapbox harangue.

"And you," Abbie said, nodding to the girl on the sofa. "What's your name?"

"Clara," the girl whispered through a veil of protective hair.

"Are you all right, Clara?"

"Yes, ma'am," Clara said under her breath. She

looked healthy—uncomfortable, but calm and pink. "I am now."

"Now?" Abbie asked.

"Yes," Clara said, looking at Doctor Gracie. "She saved me, Doctor Gracie did. I was in no position to have a child, and with the new laws—"

"Laws that are in place for a reason," her partner spat. "You're a murderer," he said and turned a venomous eye to Doctor Gracie. "You're *both* murderers."

"Age old debate that needs no rehashing," Dr. Gracie said, dismissing the argument before it began. "That's why I operate the way I do."

"How's that?" Abbie asked, noting the doctor's hands, steady and sure, instruments of both life and death.

"It's sterile, it's safe, there's informed consent from the patient, if a reasonable age. They stay here at the cabin until they feel well enough to depart. A retreat, of sorts. That's the facade, anyhow."

A place of life restored. Saved. Not taken, Abbie thought.

Abbie looked at her partner, the lips that had spewed misogynistic rhetoric behind doors opened and closed alike, the cock of an entitled head full of tainted ideas that permeated society, stripping creatures with gash instead of shaft of control over their own flesh.

"You're a monster," he reiterated, "and a criminal. Your little operation is officially closed for business."

Abbie watched him, his hands reaching for the cold, steel cuffs on his belt, hands she had never welcomed but had felt nonetheless. Groping, assaulting, controlling ...

She heard him—his vile words, words that had cut her gender so many times before, reducing women to no more than incubators and servants.

It felt good, the cold steel in her hand vibrating from the ejaculation of death. It was beautiful, the crimson release seeping from the hole in her partner's head.

Clara's hands shrouded her face, and her gasp caught in the ringing aftershock of the gun's discharge. Doctor Gracie was as she had been, sitting proud, head held high; the only difference was she was no longer wringing her hands.

"Here, let me help you clean this up," Abbie said, assessing the splatter of blood and brains.

"No, my dear," Dr. Gracie said, a squinting smile scrunching her already prominent wrinkles into welcoming crevices. "I'll clean up the bloody fool. I have the means and knowledge ..." Her eyes shifted to Clara.

It felt better than good, the freedom Abbie granted Doctor Gracie. Clara. *The girls, the women… herself.* Though small in scope, it was something. A shallow breath back into the lungs of civil, respectful humanity. Abbie stepped forward and kissed the old woman on the cheek.

"Carry on," Abbie said, holstering her weapon and walking out the door.

melissa taveras

Melissa Taveras is a writer and poet who is Marine Corps veteran and graduate of American Intercontinental University.

She is currently working on her first novel and hopes to continue contributing to feminism and the MMIW/MMIP movement through her poetry.

She has Native American, African and European ancestry and was raised in a traditional Dominican American culture.

She is a fierce feminist and feels the need to use her voice to uplift others.

joy kennedy-o'neill

Joy Kennedy-O'Neill's fiction has appeared in *Strange Horizons*, *Daily Science Fiction*, *Galaxy's Edge*, *The Cimarron Review*, *Flash Fiction Online*, and more. Joy teaches English for a small college on the Texas coast. She enjoys sunny days, cheese, and bouts of sincere awkwardness. Find her at JoyKennedyOneill.com.

chantell renee

Chantell enjoys writing for a large range of genres, from Horror to Romance, with a shadow of darkness in every story. She's been published by five different small presses, and her own small press, Limitless Ink. She's appeared at multiple conventions as well as Barnes & Noble stores throughout Houston. She has also sat on panels for Barnes & Nobles, and for the Bayou City Book Festival and Comicpalooza. She is a musician, artist, writes for the House of Stichted magazine and is part of a duo on the Sex and Horror Podcast.

jennifer schomburg kanke

Jennifer Schomburg Kanke, originally from Columbus, Ohio, lives in Tallahassee, Florida, where she edits confidential documents for the government. Her work has appeared in *Goblin Fruit, Gingerbread House, and NonBinary Review*. She is a previous winner of the Science Fiction Poetry Association's annual contest. Her chapbook, *Fine, Considering*, about her experiences undergoing chemotherapy for ovarian cancer, is available from Rinky Dink Press. She serves as instructional support for Annie Finch's self-paced course in metrical poetry, A Poet's Ear, available at www.poetrywitch.org

jason myers

Jason Myers grew up in Northwest Ohio. Avid reader for years he put aside his dreams of writing to raise his children and focus on being an EMT/Firefighter. He has been published in horror anthologies as well as several novellas of his own. He is the co-author of the Eternal Sisterhood Series with RJ Roles. RJ and Jason have since founded Crimson Pinnacle Press, a publishing company that deals with horror and the macabre. Active member of the Horror Authors Guild, he currently resides and still serves his city on the fire department in Maumee, Ohio.

julie harding

Julie Harding is a teacher and writer who lives in New Jersey with her husband and two sons. She loves telling people what to read next and aspires to make the perfect cup of coffee, commit to exercising daily, and publish a novel.

shawn w. foley

Shawn is lucky enough to share is passion for horror books and movies with his wife and two sons. A research scientist by day, he escapes into worlds of zombies, ghosts, and monsters in his spare time. His work has been included in episodes of *The No Sleep Podcast* and *Tales to Terrify* podcast. He is honored to be included in the *Open Your Mouth* anthology.

donelle pardee whiting

Donelle Pardee Whiting is an experienced writer, editor, and photographer. Her interest in the dark, creepy, and occasionally macabre brought her to Stitched Smile Publications at its beginning. She uses her experience, skills, and dedication to the craft—along with a degree in journalism and time in the newspaper trenches—as the content editor for Stitched Smile Publications and the Managing Editor of *House of Stitched* Magazine.

Donelle lives in Central Illinois with her husband Christian and their two dogs, Polly the Not-a-Husky and Clara the Wonder Husky.

patricia flaherty pagan

Patricia Flaherty Pagan, MFA has published award-winning horror, crime, and literary short fiction and poetry in a range of journals and anthologies. In addition to authoring *Enduring Spirit: Stories*, she has edited anthologies such as *Eve's Requiem: Tales of Women, Mystery and Horror*. She teaches short fiction writing at Writespace Houston. Learn more about her books, writing workshops, and developmental editing services at www.patriciaflahertypagan.com. Follow her on twitter @PFwriteright and on Instagram @patriciaflahertypaganauthor.

melissa algood

Melissa is an award-winning author of many stories and books. Her hometown, Annapolis, inspired the setting of *Everything That Counts*, a coming-of-age story of a geek who yearns to be cool. *The Greater Good* series follows a blood-thirsty assassin and her ex-Navy S.E.A.L. handler; the three-book series has a body count which matches the make-out count. Her award-winning short fiction can be found in *Everyone Dies: Tales from a Morbid Author*.

Melissa's moved over twenty times in her life, including California, Puerto Rico, and D.C., before making Houston her home. She's a hairstylist in the 'real' world and lives with her longtime love, Izzy, and Madame Bijou, their tuxedo cat.

jessica raney

Jessica Raney is the author of seven books. Her latest, *Rack and Ruin* is the final book in her Appalachian-Supernatural-Noir series. Her other works include a zombie Apocalypse adventure, *These Violent Delights*, and two collections of short stories, *Oddballs* and *Dreadful Pennies*. Her style could be best described as the intersection of dark comedy, horror, and the fantastical. Originally from southern Ohio, Jessica now lives in Houston, Texas.

chris mcauley

A writer who specializes in the Horror, Science Fiction and crime genre. Chris has been the lead writer in novels, comics, audio dramas and games. He is the co-creator of the popular StokerVerse, along with Bram Stoker's great-grand nephew Dacre Stoker. He has also created a science fiction and fantasy franchise with Babylon 5's Claudia Christian. Chris has worked with some of the top names in Star Wars, Star Trek and Doctor Who.

j.l. henker

J.L. lives in Northern California with her spouse, Diane, and a red tabby named Leo. Primarily a fiction writer, she is working on a fantasy novel, outlining a space opera and submitting speculative fiction short stories for publication. She is also a blogger and publishes a quarterly newsletter. As a former used/rare book buyer for a local bookstore, she uses her experience in valuing old/rare books as a volunteer with the local Friends of the Library.

Website: https://jlhenker.com

jae mazer

Jae Mazer was born in Victoria, British Columbia, and grew up in the prairies of Northern Alberta. After spending the majority of her life battling sasquatches in the Great White North, she migrated south to Texas to have a go at the armadillos. Jae always had an obsession with reading and inherited a love of all things dark and horror from her dad. One day, she decided that she had devoured enough words that she could spin a decent yarn of her own. Now she is an award-winning author with a dozen novels under her belt, short stories in various publications, and is an affiliate member of the Horror Writers Association.

lisa vasquez

By her "Darque Design," Lisa Vasquez creates vivid, twisted horror with the precision of a scalpel. Lisa's writing style has been compared to the works of Mary Shelley, Baz Luhrman, and the Grand Guignol, and is hailed as a writer of nightmarish vision and poetic voice in today's horror genre.

Lisa is the CEO of Stitched Smile Publications, Editor-in-Chief of House of Stitched Magazine, the owner of Darque Halo Designs (book covers), Unsaintly Art Studios (Freelance Artwork) and also volunteers as a mentor to other authors.